Enclosed Love
Sexy
Stories
Collection

VOLUME 21

10 EROTIC SHORT STORIES

DAKOTA DEECE

Publisher's Note: This is a work of fiction. Names,
characters, places, and incidents are a product of
the author's imagination. Locales and public
names are sometimes used for atmospheric
purposes. Any resemblance to actual people, living
or dead, or to businesses, companies, events,
institutions, or locales is completely coincidental.

Enclosed Love/ Dakota Deece. -- 1st ed.
Xplicit Press, an imprint of TLM Media LLC

ISBN-13: 978-1-62327-552-5
ISBN-10: 1-62327-552-0
eISBN 978-1-62327-602-7

Printed in the United States of America

CONTENTS

1 SNOWED IN

The sound of the snow smacking over the edge of the cabin woke her from a terrifying dream. The vestiges remained for a few seconds of heart-stopping terror, before she realized where she was.

"It's amazing what your brain does to you at night," she snorted.

There were dark shadows all around her. The hut she'd collapsed into after struggling through the blizzard was a dark one, but she couldn't hear anyone else around her, though the walls and roof creaked ominously.

She groaned, sat up and looked around. The tiny room's windows were blanketed in white and grey—the snow was either very deep or was clinging to them. The last thing she wanted was to be snowed in forever, and as soon as that window gave way, she knew she'd be in deep trouble. She sat still for a few minutes and then reached over to her backpack, which she'd used as a pillow, and rummaged to take stock. She had enough food to last maybe a day, perhaps more. She figured that she might have to dig her way out though, which was something she wasn't looking forward to. There was a commotion outside the hut. A thumping on the roof, and a voice, muffled to an inaudible murmur. She could hear someone though.

"Hello!" she shouted—reprieve and fear vying for attention in her stomach and voice. Fear won her body, while liberation took her mind; the shaky feeling from being both heady and chilly at the same time. She rushed to the door, opening it to find a wall of snow up to most of the way over the door. The voice called again. "Anyone in there?" a male voice called, and she clapped her hands delightedly.

"YES!" she yelled. "I'm in here, can you help me?"

"Any injuries?" he asked, and she sighed, relaxing as relief washed over her.

"No. But I'm going to have to dig my way out," she said.

"Yeah, that happens a lot here," he said, and suddenly, a head was leaning down over the edge of the roof. Piercing blue eyes swept over her, and then he said, "Start digging a bit—you can use the snow to make water if you put it in the pot over the fire, and I'll dig from the other side. We'll have to hole up here for a while—there's another storm heading this way, but we should be able to manage just fine. I'll clear the chimney too, give me a few minutes."

She heard him scraping around above her, and she dived back to her pack, grabbed a hairband, pulled her black hair into a messy ponytail, and took her mini shovel out of the pack. She rushed over to the fireplace, and grabbed the massive pot, which was hanging from a pole over the fire, and carefully filled it with snow.

Then she returned to the fireplace. Dim light was filtering in through the window beside her—she could see him sweeping the snow off of the ones in the roof, so she could see better.

She looked around, and made a cozy fire, placing the pan carefully back above it.

After a few minutes, he came and joined her, and she looked over at him nervously. He was stamping snow off his feet, and had almost slid in, down an embankment of packed snow and through the door. She threw more wood on the fire, and went back to her sleeping bag, to sit down.

The man stripped layer after layer of clothes until he was down to a t-shirt and warm trousers. His muscles gleamed in the firelight and she gasped.

"Jack!?" she said with a horrified, embarrassed grin. Jack was the part-time ranger—the one that had given her the very map she'd used to find the hut. He laughed softly.

"Well, well, it's Jess, isn't it?" She nodded her head, startled and dumbstruck. He laughed again, "I never expected to find you here," he continued, and looked around. The fire was heating the room nicely, but the heat rising in her cheeks was something else entirely. He looked almost good enough to devour, whole.

He approached her, sitting down across from her after spreading out his own sleeping bag. "I guess there are far worse ways to be stuck in a storm," he said with a grin and she smiled back.

She wasn't quite sure how it happened. One minute, she was nibbling on some food that they'd cooked, and the next, she was being kissed passionately. She responded in kind, her hand coming up unconsciously to cling to his neck as he ravaged her, rolling kisses all the way down from the corner of her mouth to the deep v in her t-shirt.

"Sorry, I've wanted to do that forever," he said, with a wicked grin as she pushed him away. She looked at him, confused, for a minute, and then he ran his tongue across his lips. "I'm sorry if I startled you," he began, and she moved to meet him, stopping his words with a needy, deep kiss. Clothes flew everywhere as they stripped—till they were down to their underwear. Practical bra and panties for her, but he gazed over her body like she was an underwear model. She was pleasantly surprised to see he went commando.

Her hands reached for him, pulling him close as they tumbled onto the sleeping bags, and using wandering fingers, she probed and tested his muscles. Her fingers slid over his chest as he lowered his mouth to take one nipple into his mouth through the fabric of her bra. He reached behind her, pulling at the clasp before sliding it down carefully, taking her nipple into his mouth again once it was bare. He ran his tongue over it, rolling it around between his teeth carefully. The intense pleasure made her wet, and she gently pushed his hand down to feel how silky and damp she was, waiting for him. He groaned again, his hands slipping deftly into her cunt, teasing and tantalizing her clitoris as he slid in and out, exploring her curves and contours.

She gasped, reaching down for his member and began stroking—her hands sliding up and down slowly. He gasped a little, as she shoved his hand aside and took some of her wetness and rubbed it on his cock, making him wet and the friction even better. She increased the speed and force, gently at first, and then with increasing speed, before he gasped, "Enough, please!"

His tongue flicked over one nipple, then the other, taking each in his mouth and hardening them as if there was a chill in the air, and she returned the favor, dipping her head to his chest, running a tongue over each nipple as he shuddered.

He murmured something into her chest then raised his head and said, "Oh god, I want you."

She laughed softly. "I want you too," which quickly turned to a yelp as his fingers slid into her panties, and began to caress and stroke her clitoris. She gasped louder, and moaned his name, as she rocked back and forward against his hands. She moaned and caressed his penis, before pulling him down onto her. He pulled back, fishing out a condom and she grinned wickedly.

"Give me it," she said, gesturing. He looked at her quizzically, and then smiled, handing it over.

She pulled it from the packet and carefully set it between her lips, moving and twisting so that she could lower her mouth to his head. She slowly slid the condom over his penis, and he struggled to retain control—the feel of her silken mouth sliding the condom down over him was almost too much. She slowed down, enjoying every muscle twitch—she was in control now. Once the condom was on, she gave him a minute to relax again and then pulled him into her.

He couldn't take it any longer and plunged in and out, the force of his slide causing her to yelp, groan and scream out his name. He kept rocking, as he felt her entire body tighten around him, the delicious silken shift in and out giving her pleasured mewls volume as he drove her closer and closer to cumming.

And then, just as she was about to cum all over him, he stopped and smiled at her.

"Oh, why did you stop," she cried, and he grinned, a wicked smile on his lips.

"I like doing this to you," he said simply, and she pulled him in tightly, as he slid a finger down over her clitoris again. Intense waves of passion followed the gentle rocking motion he built up on her clitoris—more intense than cumming all over him while being fucked. She couldn't believe it, the waves and crescendos taking her higher and higher, but still not over the edge.

He kept her there expertly, fingers working her clitoris, and gently rocking in and out of her until he could take it no more and drove into her. She exploded, a scream of pleasure marking the beginning of waves of passion as they tumbled from her. He came too, his body convulsing, shivering, and jerking as the fire burned through and out of him. He enjoyed the feel of her pulsing around him, and they lay, sweating and exhausted, for a minute before he laughed softly, and said:

"Thank you..."

"You're welcome," she said with a grin.

In the morning, when he got up, he said, "Same time next storm?"

She grinned, "See you here!"

2 ENCLOSED SPACES

"**M**iss Cartwright, I require a taxi in half an hour, can you arrange that please?" came the voice over her boss's intercom. Rita sighed—it wasn't a request. She would suffer if she didn't deliver the expected taxi. And sometimes, just occasionally, she wished she could make HIM suffer. It was a happy fantasy, one that caused her to snap one stocking strap through her skirt, relishing the slap against her skin.

"Oh, and please accompany me down—I have some notes that I need dictated and typed up, though they won't take long—best to do so in the elevator, I feel," he added and she rolled her eyes. She frequently ended up getting in the taxi with him, with nothing more than a notepad and pen. Once she'd been practically stranded at Heathrow, until she'd called another staff member and had them send one of the company cars. Everett had been pissed off at that—and had threatened to dock her pay if it happened again.

"A secretary should always be prepared," she mimicked in a sing-song voice, slamming a drawer out of the way and closing everything down. She grabbed her handbag, checked to make sure she had her Oyster card, and then phoned Everett's favorite cab firm.

It wasn't as if he was really important, she mused, looking around the office. He was a mid-level sales executive and only had a secretary because he was the nephew of the company's owner. He'd been stuck down here as a gesture—there wasn't anything spectacular about him—or at least, not that she'd seen in the last few weeks. It was incredible to think that they would be even considering working together in another year's time, but his department had been ring-fenced, as Everett had always crowed after meetings.

The taxi arrived twenty minutes later—Everett swept through Rita's office and gestured imperiously with one finger. "Take this down please, Miss Cartwright," he said and began to fire off instructions. And it was then she realized something—he was going away on holiday! She couldn't believe her luck. Two weeks of peace and quiet—and perhaps a little time off herself.

They reached the elevator—it was an old and cranky piece of machinery, which often creaked and moaned. Though they were nine floors up, Rita preferred the stairs—her toned legs were testament to her fear of "coffin boxes" as her brother had once called them, much to her bemusement. Everett though? Preferred them and would not climb stairs even if the elevator were broken. He'd even flat-out refused and gone home once.

"Miss Cartwright," he snapped and she blinked. "Did you hear what I just said?"

She wanted to complain, but there was something about him that told her she shouldn't. "No sir, sorry sir; I think

I might have a migraine coming on."

He snorted. "I was saying, you can have next week off—it's not as if we'll need you here, and it's a waste to keep you at your desk if people can leave messages with the switchboard." She resisted grinning, as he continued, "Just accompany me to Heathrow, and you're free to leave from there."

She waited until he turned his back then rolled her eyes. Heathrow! In London traffic at rush hour, she'd be lucky to see her home before 8 pm. Still. A week of vacation?

The elevator creaked to a stop and the doors opened, though they had to step down into it.

"Make a note to let them know about this before we leave," Everett said, almost automatically then blinked. "On second thought, I'll deal with it when we get to the foyer. This building is maintained so badly, I think I might have to pursue it with my uncle later."

"Yes sir," Rita said and leaned forward to push the button. They'd travelled less than two floors when the elevator stopped suddenly. She jerked off her feet into Everett—he caught her, putting his hands around her waist.

They shared a look; she twisted to look over her shoulder, before he hastily let go, his face turning slightly red.

"It broke?" he said, incredulously. Rita tilted her head and shrugged.

"Fix it!" he demanded. She choked back a laugh.

"What do you expect me to do, sir? Wave a magic secretarial wand?"

Instead, she reached forward and pressed the bell. Nothing happened. She sighed.

Reaching into her purse, she pulled out a mobile phone and looked.

"No signal," she murmured. Everett stamped his foot, and she turned around. He was actually shaking and loosening his tie.

"This is unacceptable, an unacceptable state of affairs," he groaned under his breath.

"Everett, stop it," Rita said and he blinked.

"Are you telling ME what to do?" he said.

She swallowed hard and said, "Yes. Yes I am. If you're not capable of remaining calm, I will tell you what to do, and you'll do it."

"Yes ma'am," he said meekly, after a

time.

She quirked an eyebrow. This might actually work. Amazingly, he was quieting down into one corner. She loosened the top button of her shirt—it was so hot in the elevator; she couldn't believe it. His eyes widened as she turned to him, and a naughty thought crossed her mind.

"Do you like to be told what to do Everett?"

"Pardon?"

"Well, you're all about control. We're going to be stuck here...for a while." His eyes widened in terror. "So, if I tell you what to do..." This was said with a wicked smile. He nodded, confused.

"First, I am Mistress," she said. His eyes widened further. "Say it!" she demanded, slipping her skirt up to show one stocking. He swallowed hard.

"Yes Mistress," he said meekly. What she wouldn't have done for her cat o-nine tails right now!

"You have three minutes to bare a piece of skin to my mouth," she said, licking her lips. "As you followed orders right away, I will let YOU choose which part to bare. But if I am dissatisfied, I will bite instead of lick," she said, while trailing her eyes lazily down to the zip of his pants. He swallowed again, then boldly licked his own lips, undid his belt, and unzipped himself. A white bulge of cloth appeared at his hand. She smiled.

"You're not 'bare' Everett," she said, hiking her skirt up around her waist to kneel better. He pulled his boxer shorts aside, his head twitching out of his pants on command.

"Well done," she said, and smiled.

"Thank you Mistress," he said dutifully. This was getting better and better.

Reaching into her handbag, she fished out a condom, and carefully peeled the package. Everett was watching, dark eyes cloudy and shocked, as if he thought this were some sort of hallucination. First, she ran a carefully trimmed nail (so that she could type) across the top of his penis, from the root, in his dark hair (which she was unsurprised to note had grey hairs), back to the tip, which twitched agonizingly. She could see him tense—but underneath his suit, it appeared, Everett was quite fit. Muscle lines at his thighs and the flat stomach she could see from her perspective looked good enough to lick and tease with her tongue. Instead, she carefully slipped the condom tip over his twitching head and, with a smooth movement, slid the whole thing onto his penis with her mouth. She waited as he groaned, and then withdrew it, standing up and looking him in the eye.

"I have not given you permission to come. If you do, I will be displeased," she added with a malicious grin. He looked straight ahead.

She was glad that there were no working cameras in this elevator—this wouldn't go down well with the owners of the building. Everett was putty in her hands and was resolutely trying to behave himself—making her wonder if he'd encountered a dom before. But, who cared. She could teach him a thing or two. And she was in control.

She licked the shaft of his cock, from root to the very tip and Everett groaned softly.

"You may vocalize," she said.

"Thank you, Miss..."

Her mouth suddenly enclosed the tip of his cock, flicking over it with her tongue as the warmth surrounded him. He leaned into the wall, his knees buckling slightly. The loud groan told her he was enjoying what she was doing to him, condom or otherwise. Caressing, and stroking, she began slowly moving her head, taking him deeper and deeper into her mouth. He was groaning and gently running his fingers through her hair, pulling it free of the low bun she wore.

She could feel him shaking under her hands, trembling and trying not to come and explode into her mouth—the tense lines of his thighs and the quavering muscles holding him up told her that he was close. Slowly, she withdrew his cock from her mouth, licking and spiraling around as she went. He gasped as she let him go, springing and wobbling, his knees almost buckling. The elevator shuddered once.

"You may...," she said, stroking him hard, "come now." With a grunt and a moan, he shuddered under her hand, leaning into her shoulder.

"Thank you Mistress" he whispered.

The elevator gave an almighty jerk and he blinked, dazed, then quickly rearranged himself, carefully pulling his pants up. She straightened her skirt, and the elevator began to move again.

They reached the bottom, and she smiled over her shoulder at him, sweeping over his flushed face with a smile.

"Next time, would you like to be my master?"

3 UNDER THE STARS

Jeanette glanced over at her fiancé and smiled. Her lip curled slightly, turning from a smile to a mocking snarl.

"This is your idea of a romantic getaway?"

Mac inclined his head, one blond curl falling into his eye. With a sweep of his hand, he removed it and gestured around the field. All she could see at first was snow. They were in a clearing, the moonlight washing over the tops of snow-covered trees. A solitary lump in the middle of the glade, like a snow-covered fairy mound, stood out and up – a hump in the middle of the snow.

"Camping babe," he said with a smile. Gesturing around, "You said you wanted to get away. I thought we could camp where we first met. I did have to work with the weather," he added, laughing softly.

"Where's the tent, asshole?" she said, her voice desperate and angry. Her teeth were chattering, and she was stamping her feet.

"Under that lump?" he said, gesturing towards it. She sighed.

"Home please."

"No – let's go and see if we can dig it out."

He kicked at the tent and some snow shifted and fanned off the other side. It was amazing to watch but, at the same time, she was angry. Angry enough to walk away. She could just hop into her car and head home. It wouldn't be difficult at all. But she really wanted him – she could always rely on him to wind her up right when she didn't expect it.

"Bastard," she hissed, then kicked the snow.

He reached over and stroked her leg. She shivered, not because of the cold –

instead, a deep need took her. It settled in her stomach, the tingle making her clench, tighten, and wiggle. He grinned, enjoying her delicious discomfort.

"Seriously, let's dig this out and then we'll see what we can do."

Ten hot, sweaty minutes later, he'd finished digging out the tent. She stomped and stamped the snow down around it, listening to the distant wolf howls and the closer crack snaps of the trees around them. She sighed. A loud crack near her made her jump and spin – hair whipping around and slapping her across the other cheek. She squeaked.

"What?" Mac said, distracted.

"Noises," she whispered in a low voice. He laughed softly.

"Yes sweet, there are noises out here. You'll find that. We're in the middle of the woods," he said sarcastically.

He went back to checking the last of the kit. She could see him spreading blankets and sheets out inside. She peeked her head in. A sheepskin rug and some sleeping bags made up the majority of the space. He laughed, looked up, and then zipped the inner door, telling her "You can look when you come in. Get your shoes unlaced though, so you're not tracking in snow…"

She did as he asked, undoing her laces and slipping straight back into her gloves.

She continued stamping her feet outside the tent, slowly circling around the clearing, keeping an eye on as much as she could. He laughed and pulled her into the tent, zipping closed the little area that acted as a porch.

It wasn't as cold in there, but still chilly. He smiled and said, "Strip!" She smiled back, kneeling instead of crouching in the room.

She shook her head. "You first!"

He laughed again, pulling off all of his clothes. He pulled everything off in sets – his trousers first, along with his thermals and socks, then all of his tops – tossing them towards the door in a small pile. She followed suit, stripping out of the clothes that she was wearing – down to her long johns. He grinned again, "All of them…."

☙❦

Jeanette sighed. She was kneeling, so she slid her top up over her head, and as she did, he moved towards her. She felt his warm mouth closing over one nipple as she struggled with her top. She shivered again and knelt back on her haunches. His hand slipped into her long, warm leggings and between her legs. She clenched her thighs tightly, trapping his hand. He laughed as she pulled her top up and off her head. His mouth let go of her nipple and joined hers, hungrily pushing his tongue into her mouth, licking her teeth and lips until she groaned and shuddered.

Her hands dropped to his waist, reaching for his cock and stroking it. Soft at first, then harder, and it was his turn to groan. His fingers found the damp space between her legs and began stroking her clitoris. She straightened again, her hands letting go of his balls and cock, and stripped to her knees, moving her thermals down to the floor.

He laid her down, his hands exploring her body, pausing to stroke her scarred hip where she'd skinned herself on the way up. She gasped slightly, pulling his fingers away and nudging them back to the deep, damp "v" between her legs. He pulled her thermals all the way off, tossing them in a heap on the floor.

His hands explored her body, stroking her as lightly as possible, the cold air following and kissing her skin, making her tremble under his hands. Then he dipped back into her core, tormenting her with his nimble fingers, nibbling her ear, her neck, and her nipples until she begged him to take her. He pulled a sleeping bag over them and carefully tore into a condom package before sliding it onto his cock with an attentive smile.

She quirked an eyebrow at him.

"You know me, safety first," he said before teasing her with his cock, using it to rub her clitoris again. She gasped and moaned, begging him to slide into her. She arched into him, her mouth hungrily licking and stroking his nipples, switching from one to the other.

There was a howl outside close to the tent, and they both froze, looking over at the tent entrance. There was a sniffling, snuffling sound outside the zipped entrance, a shadow looming. They held onto one another until the snuffling moved away. Mac broke the silence first, laughing while dipping back into her wet, chilled core. She soon heated up and he was slipping into her gently, his hands pulling her hips close.

Jeanette had other ideas though; she wanted to feel Mac in her mouth. She ducked her head, moving her fingers down over the hair at the root of his cock, her mouth seeking his hard shaft, taking it into her mouth as he groaned and arched his back. Her tongue rolled around it while she held it in her mouth. A smile spread across his face as he said softly, "I love it when you blow me."

She cradled his balls in her hands, stroking the skin behind it, then taking him further into her mouth, his cock pushing into her throat. She slipped him in and out, moving him carefully, bobbing her head and licking him up and down like a lollipop. He groaned again, louder, burying his hands in her hair, muscles tightening as she led him closer and closer to cumming. She took him right to the edge as he thrust into her, then let go and back out of her mouth, and withdrew. For a minute, he kept his eyes closed, every muscle line taut and tight as he tried to stop himself from cumming. She smiled and drew back a little more, wide eyes taking in everything that he was doing. She ran her fingers along his skin – along the tight, taut lines at the edges of his thighs. Her fingers explored muscles that were rock-hard and tense, enjoying the feel of his control and struggling to keep it under her fingers. Soon when he was a bit calmer, he moved over, shuffling towards her before dipping back into her – she was hot, wet, and desperately waiting for him.

A long slide and he was in her, rocking backwards and forwards as he brought her to the edge of her climax. With each stroke, she tightened around him, until she was snug and close to him, clutching onto him as he rocked into her. His mouth explored her neck and caught one nipple after another as she moved and bucked and twisted beneath him. He was clinging to her too, his head buried in one sweet spot in her neck, pumping into her as she whimpered and yelped. He smiled, letting her cool off before pushing her onto her back, then sliding back into her again.

Her yelps were louder, begging, moving up to him as he slammed down. He slid into her hard, fucking her as fast as he could. She squealed and writhed underneath him, clutching him tighter as she came around him, screaming his name. He kept pumping, rocking in and out as she moved with him. He came a few seconds later, burying his face in her chest, crying out hoarsely.

After pulling out and throwing the condom out – putting it in a bag and into the outside porch – they snuggled into one another, kissing and murmuring.

"Mmmm, I think I like this camping after all," Jeanette said as Mac turned out the lights.

4 BOUNTY HUNTING

Two bounty hunters take down their most satisfying hunt—each other.

A dart rocketed past her head with a low whistle. She sucked in a breath, surprised, and looked around trying to see where it came from. She ducked behind the low wall beside her, waiting breathlessly as no further darts or whistles shot by her. She looked around the edge of the wall and couldn't see anything.

She moved quickly, ducking into an alcove. Another dart bounced at her feet. She sighed. It might be a big game for them, but it was still something that he took far too seriously—he was using anesthetic darts again.

"Your shot is lousy," she called to the air around her. Another dart smacked at waist height, about three inches from her ass. She bent over and waved her butt at the building across the way, knowing he'd have to reload, and then darted back into cover.

It wasn't as if they were actually hunting one another or to shoot to kill—still, she didn't like the darts, and though he knew that fine, well, he was doing it deliberately.

Just one of those things, she thought, trying to work out roughly where he was by the bouncing darts following behind her heels like a nipping dog.

Finally, she gained the cool, safe cover of another bigger building and turned the corner to the stairs to find a glass of champagne, the beads of water clinging to it with the note "drink me" in front of her on the stairs. One of their rules was that gifts could be trusted—there was no drugging of food or drink allowed.

She picked it up, looking around furtively, then closed her eyes and enjoyed a sip of it, then another, before carefully replacing it on one of the nearby outcrops of brick. This staircase looked newer—she assumed that the jutting bricks were the old spiral staircase. It made a handy shelf for her glass.

She slowly crept up the stairs, which spiraled around and up and over her head. She knew he might be waiting there, though she hoped he would have abandoned his dart gun.

She quite enjoyed the pain of it all, of course. Whether supplying or receiving, there was something that she just couldn't explain about having him spank her or tie her up or shoot her with a tazer to capture her. She knew it was deviant, but she really didn't care. All she wanted was the thrill of the hunt, outsmarting him so she could dominate. If he captured her, she'd have to submit to his will.

They'd met years ago, at a convention for bodyguards. At the time, she'd found him attractive, but as the years passed, he grew even more so. Subjugating her to his will was something that made her tingle and buck as if he'd jolted her with a shock. It was amazing. The deep passion that moved between them was incredible, indescribable.

Today though, today, she wanted to be the dominant partner. She knew that if he swung back to check the champagne, he'd know she'd passed through. But he had to get behind her first, which wasn't as easy as it sounded. The maze of warrens and warehouse fronts that they played in were deserted and nonsensical. Locked doors that stood the test of time while others crumbled meant that instead of playing in an open area, they were chasing one another around a labyrinthine area with dead ends and sheer drops as walkways and platforms crumbled under the weight of desertion.

She knew that his only option to get to where he was firing for her, without scaling walls with a rope, was to head this way and that at the end of this walkway, just beyond where he fired from, twisted and melted metal marked the end of a path. That area was charred and burned after a fire ripped through the building—some of it remained safe, while the rest of it was precarious and impassable. So, as long as he didn't get the jump on him, she could corner him and have her way with him.

She stripped out of her leather top, revealing a lacy quarter bra and then dropped it behind her, slinking along the walkway. She kept a hold of her stun gun, but by now, he would be as frustrated as she was and would agree to almost anything. This was the fun part.

She found him on one of the bigger platforms, a hammock spread between the two apex corners over one edge, stripped to the waist, waiting patiently. As she rounded the corner, he grinned.

"Out of ammo," he said, gesturing at his discarded gun.

"You're...spent?" she replied, echoing his grin. He laughed softly. "So, I win?" she continued and he nodded his head.

"Looks that way, doesn't it?" he said with a smile. He stripped off his shorts, his erection standing up as soon as he did. She grinned some more.

"What if I don't want to fuck you?" she asked. He shrugged.

"Your wish is my command," he said. "But I'd be very sad if you didn't."

Her grin was unrepentant, as she

stripped of her skin-tight leather trousers. She wasn't wearing anything underneath and he groaned.

"I want you," he demanded. She laughed.

"Beg, dog," she said, playing with her nipples and looking at him from under her eyelashes. Her hand trailed down to her stomach and then rapidly dipped between her legs, finding her clit. He gasped and groaned, his own hands slipping to his cock.

"No," she said, "you watch. You don't touch me...or yourself."

He groaned again and then put his hands up behind the head. She scooted past him, to the head of the hammock and whipped out a set of handcuffs, attaching him to the wide loop, which held up one end of the hammock with ease.

"Ooh," he said, trying to lift up to lick part of her skin as she bent over him, "That's not fair!"

Silvery laughter echoed out, as she brought one finger down for him to taste her—and he shuddered again, his erection twitching in the air. She laughed and pulled back, kneeling over him in the hammock after a brief wiggle. The cuffs tinkled and sang in the still night air around them.

Her hands moved down her skin again, stroking down the insides of her thighs, bending slightly, and her breasts moved down, closer to him. Her long hair tickled his chest as she bent to put her fingers inside herself. He groaned, arching his back, and she smiled at him, leaning down to kiss him.

"Beg," she told him, sliding her fingers in and out. She ran one over her clit, rubbing hard and he sighed heavily.

"I want you," he said.

"That's not begging," she replied, between gasps of pleasure. "Be quick, if I cum before you beg, you won't have me at all," she told him and leaned back a bit, giving him a better view.

Her fingers were slick and damp, and her eyes were closed, her finger rocking back and forth over her clitoris and occasionally dipping into her core. When she did slip inside herself, she gasped and moaned his name.

"Please," he said, his voice soft and desperate.

"Still not begging," she said.

"Please, mistress."

In one swift motion, she took his cock in her hand and lowered herself onto it.

"Better," she said and began to rock back and forth. Once he was at the edge of what he could stand, she withdrew again and laughed.

"Well?" she said. He was breathing hard, panting and trying to keep himself under control. Her smooth silky movements had brought him close to the edge and left him wanting more.

"Well what?" he finally managed.

"Want your hands untied?"

"Yes please."

She reached up and flipped the catch on his handcuffs, one side then the other, before pulling them free. He laughed and hungrily reached up to pull her down on top of him. He hungrily devoured her mouth and with a soft tug, lowered her back onto his cock, arching into her as he felt her hot, sweet, dampness envelop him. His fingers reached up to her nipples and drew one then the other between them, his mouth reaching up to take one into his mouth as he lavished attention on the other. Slowly, they began to rock together, then faster. He pulled her under him, rolling so he was on top and so he could drive into her. He slammed into her as she mewled and sighed under him, her voice chiming out again and again. Calling his name, she tightened around him, her body spasming and grasping him as they moved. He kept driving, enjoying the feel of the pulses and shudders along his cock. It drove him wild as he slid into her again and again, until finally, with a shudder, he came.

They slowed, the hammock rocking beneath them as he collapsed on top of her. They lay together for a time, before she said, "next time, I want to be handcuffed."

"I'm sure that can be arranged," he said, with a contented sigh.

5 PRETTY LITTLE FLOWER

The shop had done a brisk trade today. Valentine's morning was always a bit of a rush, but by afternoon, the bell just hadn't stopped ringing. She hadn't sold out of everything, but it was close.

Jess looked around with a sigh. The shop didn't really have what she was looking for, and she really wanted some flowers to cheer herself up. She could put them on the table and pretend – just pretend – someone had bought them for her.

"Michael, are you here?" she called. Michael, her boyfriend, owned the store, but because he worked with flowers, he never brought them home. He always thought chocolates or something else would be better. Michael didn't answer, so she called again, "Michael, where are you?"

A trail of petals was strewn all over the floor, leading into the back room. It was a deliberate trail too, not random like the odd petal falling off here or there. She frowned; she was confused but followed the trail. Since she started dating him four weeks ago, he'd been pretty much the perfect gentleman. Kisses on her doorstep, though passionate, hadn't led to anything else, and she was now very confused. She couldn't work out if he liked her or not.

The flower trail of blood red rose petals led into the back of the shop. "Michael?" she called. "Come on through, Jess," she smiled softly, her eyes following the trail of petals on the ground. They led all the way through the back of the shop, to the stairs, and then started going up, the delicate cascade running in reverse up the stairs. Intermingled with them were Inca lilies, her favourite flowers, and tears sprang from her eyes. He had been listening. And she could see the proof of it in front of her.

She didn't realise that the shop had a second level; she slipped between narrow shelves lining both walls with notions and pieces to fill with flowers. Sympathy vases and nursery flower pots. Big circle rings that could be stuffed with flowers, or tiny corsage holders. On she went, following the red petals and the gold lilies, bending to pick up one or two of the perfect ones before ducking through doorways with a happy smile. She passed through two arches before she finally came upon...

A bed...covered in flowers.

"Oh wow," she said, looking around in wonderment. Michael was sitting on the end of the bed, in jeans and a tight white T-shirt, his strong arms tanned and lined, small beads of sweat rolling off his forehead. He looked flushed and flustered, but patted the bed.

"For you, my sweet," he said and held up a flute of champagne.

She gingerly crossed to him, with a soft smile.

"I thought you might like a bath, and then a meal, and then.... Well, we'll see where the night takes us," he said with a soft smile.

She could see steam curling from one side of the room, the delicious aroma of rose oil and something else sweet floating in the air. She had thought it was the steam.

Carefully, she picked her way to the bathroom and looked in. It looked so inviting, with white flowers and rose petals floating in the steaming water.

"They're jasmine," he breathed in her ear, kissing her neck. She gasped as he pulled her close to him. "And I thought, as you asked for flowers, that for Valentine's, I'd give you as many different kinds as I could...and I," he added, pulling her closer, "want you."

A coil of heat ignited in her stomach, and she gasped, her nipples growing taut suddenly. He chuckled softly and reached around her waist, untying her skirt. "If I may be so bold," he said, deft fingers pulling the tie loose. Her dress opened like a bud, exposing her bare skin and lacy figments underneath. She had hoped when she got up this morning that something might happen, but never in her wildest dreams....

He slipped the dress off her shoulders and she carefully stepped out of her shoes before turning around and meeting his gaze. He nodded appreciatively, then ran his hands over her breasts – the gentlest touch – while murmuring, "Some flowers crumple easily, and some are hardy. Which are you?" He bent, nibbling her neck, and she moaned, pulling him tighter. Laughing, he ran his hands over her back, down and around her hips before cupping her ass, the smooth silk whispering under his caress.

He hooked her panties, pulling them down, carefully sliding them over her hips and down her thighs. She kicked them off, as his hands trailed between her legs. The tickling motion was smooth and soft as he travelled between her thighs, stroking gently as he moved his hand up, burrowing in until he found her clit. Then, with a gentle flick, he began rocking his finger back and forth. Slowly at first, building friction, as his mouth began to devour her nipples through the lace and silk of her bra. She groaned, hanging onto him, and he laughed softly.

"Shall I put you in the bath and

continue?" he said, with an arched eyebrow. Jess could only nod as his fingers worked at her core. She could feel herself becoming wetter and wetter and could only manage to groan and whimper into his shoulder, the waves of pleasure rolling over her in faster and stronger slides. His finger suddenly slipped into her, invading her, and she squealed with pleasure.

"I want you. Take me," she panted, demanding and excited.

"Are you sure? That bath will go to waste," he said, mock disappointed, and then laughed. "Take me then," he said with another deep kiss. She ran her hands under his shirt, moving it up to his mid-chest, feeling the muscles underneath tipple and move, his dark chocolate skin soft and silky under her fingers. It reminded her of a rose petal rubbed between her fingers, and as she gazed up into his eyes, he grinned.

They stumbled to the bed, tripping over the raised platform the mattress lay on, landing on the edge of the bed in a rush of limbs and bare skin. He had pulled off his T-shirt in the rush to the bed, and Jess giggled delightedly, taking his nipples into her mouth, the firm edges tight and wrinkling slightly under her ministrations. He smelled so good – the alluring scent of flowers mixed with a musky, deeper scent, his sweat, beading on his skin as his heart thudded harder and harder against her lips, as she kissed deep into the collarbone. The tang there was delicious – a salty, soft taste with an undertone of flowers. It was his turn to groan, as her tongue licked in and out of the dip before trailing up to nibble his ear. Her hands sought out his penis, taking it into her hand and caressing him. He tipped his head back, a deep groan erupting from his lips as she stroked gently up and down, building speed, building friction.

It was his turn to beg. "I want you. I want you," he murmured over and over into her hair. He reached to his bedside table, took a slim silver package from the table, and moved fluidly, tearing the packet before reaching down and putting it on him. And in the next motion, he was sliding into her, as she arched her hips to meet him. They rocked and moved as one, getting used to each other's rhythms, building friction – bumping and sliding and building friction as she moved under him. She was fluid and as soft as a flower under his hands, and he could feel her body tightening around him. She moved as if she couldn't bear it, gasping and crying into his shoulder, begging him to cum.

"Cum all over me, my pretty little flower," he murmured, and Jess exploded, her orgasm slamming through her. She bucked and cried out, grasping him tighter, pulling him in, until he couldn't take it anymore, and he exploded into her – the fire pouring out as she spasmed and clenched around him, moulding her body to his. He came to a shuddering stop, still sliding in and out gently to prolong his orgasm before finally collapsing on top of her.

They collapsed onto the bed, both worn out and laughing softly, stroking each other, the tingles running through one another as they caressed and explored each other's arms and chests. He ducked his head to her nipple, and she yelped and jumped under him until she begged him to stop. He laughed, clearing a space on the bed under her, moving the flowers to either side in little mounds, erasing the pattern they'd made fucking on the bed. He rose and moved through to the bathroom, as she lay cooling herself, waving her hand over her face.

"Happy Valentine's Day," he whispered, lying back on the bed with her after a time. "I couldn't decide on which flower to get you...."

She pulled him down and silenced him with another kiss....

6 LOVE ME TONIGHT

Light fingers tickled over his skin in a breath of air coming through the window. He blew out the last candle and wished himself a happy birthday, then looked over at the photo on the mantelpiece. His eyes rested on the image of him hugging a slight blond girl before whispering, "Happy Anniversary."

He sighed. Today had been an odd day. 30th birthdays don't come around every day, obviously, but as he'd also married his wife two years ago today and she'd died soon after, he didn't know whether being happy was even appropriate. His fingers fell to the box that he'd stored meticulously, opening it to read the last notes she'd ever written to him.

Another touch of chill at his neck made him turn around and look for the source. His house wasn't drafty – far from it. He couldn't work out where the caress was coming from.

He felt as if someone was running fingers up his spine, trailing up and down like Jane used to. It used to be his most favourite sensation in the world – the best thing that he'd ever felt. Now, it just increased his disquiet.

He shivered again and moved away, taking the dishes through and washing them. Once finished, he picked up his phone, replied to a few messages, then took a bottle of beer and tried to settle and watch a program on TV. The feeling of being touched and stroked didn't diminish. In fact, it intensified as time passed. And when the sensation reached his crotch, he decided that the best thing was a cold shower.

"Mark...," a voice whispered, as he climbed into the shower.

"Who's there?" he called.

"I am," the voice replied, softly. He looked around and couldn't see anything, or anyone, the open plan studio easy to survey from the bathroom.

Shaking his head, he muttered to himself, "Jeez, I really need to lay off the beer and the maudlin thoughts."

He climbed into the shower, switching it to cold. For a minute, he thought he could see the shape of a person standing under the water before shaking his head and getting into the tub behind the flow of water.

The shower did little to quell the sensations sliding over his skin – and by the time he got into bed and tried to go to sleep, he just couldn't settle.

He could feel the chill settling over his chest and skin, tickling his nerves and tingling through him. So he sank into it, enjoying it.

Fingers rolled across his thighs, tracing his muscles and lines as a ghostly figure began to materialise around him. The face solidified and became his beloved Jane. As she dipped down to kiss him, he smiled and ran his fingers into her hair. She didn't feel quite real, but it was close.

A tear slipped from his eye, and she began to say, "No, don't cry," before his lips came up and crushed hers. His fingers ran over her back, tickling her, before caressing her skin and running his fingers over it. The more he did, the more she solidified, her skin heating under his touch, becoming more solid, more real. Soon, she was there with him, a soft grin on her face. He smiled back, tears of gratitude slipping from his eyes.

"Jane?" She reached down and placed a finger to his lips, stilling his next question.

Once she had, she trailed her finger down his chest, over his tight stomach, and circled the root of his cock, delicately smoothing the hairs under her fingers, ticking his balls. He smiled, cupping her breasts as she sat above him, his eyes widening in pleasure as she let him slide into her just once. Hot, wet and tight, he groaned and spasmed up reflexively before she got up and moved to kneel beside him.

"I've missed you," she said. "I get to see you once a year and I've MISSED you."

"What? Once a year?" he said, blinking.

"I get to see you once a year, if you like. Oh, and happy birthday."

"Thanks," he said, pulling her closer, his mouth reaching hers and licking it greedily.

His tongue invaded her mouth and licked her teeth and lips. She was still slightly cold, but he was enjoying the taste of her on his tongue. He groaned again, running his hands up her arms and rubbing her, trying to pull the chill out of his skin. She felt amazing – silky and soft as he moved closer to her, shimmying across the bed until his thigh touched her leg. He grinned again. She was as real as he was, or an amazingly realistic hallucination. Her hand reached down and caressed his balls again, his dick twitching against her inner wrist, bouncing slightly as she stroked him from root to tip. He gasped, all attention on her hands.

"Lie back and let me lavish...," she paused, dipping her head to one of his nipples, "...some attention on you," she continued, trailing a tongue down his abs and stopping at his cock.

Blowing gently, she laughed softly as his head twitched, and he shuddered again.

Her mouth enclosed him, the velvet feel of her breath enveloping him, and she gently licked once more before sucking and caressing him. One hand circled his cock just below her mouth; the other cupped his balls as she began to caress him. Long strokes, in time with her mouth, as he groaned and clenched his hands, gathering up the sheets beneath him. The feel was incredible – it had been so long since he'd felt that and Jane was very good at that.

He moved under her, trying to reach between her legs to play with her – to give her some pleasure back. He couldn't reach; she wriggled away from his hands, only giving him access to her full breasts. So he played with them instead, caressing and stroking her nipples. She groaned and kept caressing him, his hands matching the rhythm of her movements.

Soon, he gasped, "enough," sweating hard, holding his breath.

She laughed and sat up, then lay down next to him, dipping her fingers in and out of the deep "v" between her legs and groaning. She moaned, as he rolled over onto his side and began stroking her. His hands moved up and down over her skin, caressing her breasts and ducking his head towards her nipple. He took one into his mouth, sucking until it became hard in his mouth, then moving to the other. She groaned again, as his fingers joined hers, caressing and moving in and out of her hot, damp space before climbing up on top of her.

He carefully slid in and then began moving in and out, as her mouth closed around his nipple again. They rolled over and then she began moving on top of him, her breasts bouncing as she moved with him. The bed began to squeak, bouncing off the wall behind them, and she laughed softly.

He pulled her down, his mouth meeting hers hungrily. She gasped and laughed throatily, her hands sliding underneath him, pulling him closer as he rocked up into her. She began to shudder, and he whispered, "Cum for me."

She laughed, gasping and groaning, as she found his nipple again, licking and sucking on it. He gasped again, his eyes sweeping over her blond hair falling over one shoulder, gathering some of that up in his hands, feeling the silky shift of it under his fingers. His hands moved back to her breasts, cupping and rubbing them as she moved up and down on top of him, her hands pushing back against his knees as she rocked and moved with him. He slipped one hand to her clit, rubbing it gently as she moved with him. He was getting close – holding back until she came all over him.

She began to shudder and cry out, her body shaking and trembling under his hands. She gasped and laughed softly, tightening around him. At each stroke, she tightened further around him until he couldn't take it any more – he pulled her down, crushing his mouth into hers, invading her mouth with his tongue. She began to cum, her body tightening and releasing around him, and he came too – he couldn't help it. His body slammed into her again and again, spending himself into her and moving with her. They moved together until finally settling and lying still, caressing one another as they slowed to a stop. He shuddered as her mouth was around his nipples, causing him to buck and giggle with the sensation. His skin was extra sensitive, feeling like a thousand breaths were all over him, as he slowly relaxed again.

She laughed, stroking him carefully, her hands all over his body until she lay down on top of him, cuddling him gently.

"You're real?"

"If you think I am," she said.

He pushed her down onto the bed, a big grin on his face.

"Happy Anniversary," she whispered before fading into nothing again.

7 BY THE BOOK

The library was quiet, still and gloomy – the windows, though clean, didn't let in much light now that the tree was in full bloom, although, she had to admit, the scent was amazing. She sighed again, running a cloth over the antique counter, a spray of polish here and there to bring up the high shine of the wood. She was amazed that it had taken this long for the day to finish up – it seemed to drag.

She finished up quickly before slipping into the back of the library and putting on her brand-new dress: red silk, cut tight across the breasts, stomach and hips before flaring to a skirt that whirled when she spun. It was a slinky dress – one designed for the sole purpose of finally meeting her online friend.

They'd talked and talked for weeks. He finally plucked up the courage to come and meet her, and so, instead of exchanging pictures and after being vetted by the exclusive site they both used, they'd agreed to meet.

For some reason, though they'd been talking for months – had many virtual dates at libraries and other places, gone to coffee shops with their laptops and pretended the other was right across the table rather than inside each other's laptops – she felt nervous. Very nervous. Her stomach was in tight knots, her knees weak and shaky. Every noise made her wince, twitch, and jump towards the door.

Finally, he knocked.

She carefully made her way to the door, her long coat covering her dress, and opened it to meet two startlingly blue eyes and a mop of black hair. He ducked his head shyly and said softly, "I'm Peter."

"Hello Peter. How...how are you?"

she asked in return, shyly twisting her coat in her hands.

"I'm fine," he said and finally looked up. His wide blue eyes were speckled with green – in the dying light of the day, under the library's light, they almost glowed. His dark hair was almost blue black under the light and looked irresistible; she wanted to reach up and run her hands through it.

"Shall we go to dinner?" he asked and she nodded happily.

They sat, eating dinner, eating one another with their eyes; he was drinking in the long red hair, which flowed down her back and tumbled over her shoulder as she talked animatedly about literature. Her grey eyes lit up as they discussed her favorites – and talked about the things that she really enjoyed in books.

An undergrad of creative writing and psychology, he had his favorites too – and discussed them with her in a way he'd never managed with any other dates. He was just as passionate about books – maybe different ones, but still passionate nonetheless. They ate and talked, and shyly caressed one another's hands across the table. And he was sad to see it end.

She looked at him, considering what to do next. Walking out of the restaurant, he had leaned in for a quick kiss, her breath catching as he did so. It was passionate and intense, the burning desire to have him suddenly shooting through her as he touched her, twining his fingers in her long hair. He kissed her hard, flashing a tongue along her lips and causing her to groan and moan with pleasure. He could feel it in his mouth. Finally, she shyly returned the deep kisses, her tongue licking in along the edges of his lips.

"Coffee?" she finally asked, stopping again outside the library. He quirked an eyebrow.

"I have a flatmate," she said finally, "and he's not keen on other men," she added.

His eyebrow dropped and he began to frown.

"You live with another man?"

"Yeah, my brother," she said, reluctantly. He laughed.

"Fair enough."

"But I can give you coffee here, if you like," she continued, stroking his arm and twisting slightly towards the door. She pulled away and he pulled her back, running his hands up her back and pulling her close.

"Don't like coffee. Do you have any tea?"

They sat in the little house above the library – the granny flat she sometimes used when she'd worked late and couldn't or wouldn't walk home for the times she was trapped in the library after freak snowstorms and other reasons. Now though, it seemed tiny, intimate, and close, as he pulled her coat off her.

He found somewhere to put it and then stood back to admire her – admire her in her new red dress, gazing down at her into the deep V at the front of her dress. Pulling her close, he nibbled her ear and whispered, "Is there a bed here?"

She nodded and pulled him towards the back door of the library and up the stairs. A small, queen-sized bed with basic blankets took up the whole top floor, the bank of windows looking down on the library below. He slipped his hands down the sides of her dress, catching the zip on one side and pulling it down as he did so. She gasped.

"Too fast?" he asked and she shook her head. She crossed to the fridge, shrugging out of her dress as she went. He smiled as she pulled out a chilled bottle of wine and picked up some glasses.

"It's usually for our book club," she explained with a shrug. Her bra and panties were scraps of lace against her pale white skin, the pink thread standing out as she walked and moved. He waited patiently until she brought him a glass of wine and then pulled her onto the bed, gasping as his hands met her ribcage and slid up to her breasts. The lace was surprisingly soft underneath, the bare whisper of it under her hands causing him to shiver. His mouth lowered, sucking a nipple through the wispy material. She shivered and shuddered, falling under him as he did so. He was still in his shirt, so she slipped her hands into his waistband and pulled his shirt free, unbuttoning it up the front until she had access to his bare skin.

Her mouth met his nipple and he gasped, arching his back. He unhooked her bra after a little bit of fumbling, then smiled at her.

"First time, wooo!" he said and she laughed. He got harder hearing that – she made him so excited he couldn't bear it. Her panties were slightly more difficult, so he stripped off his jeans and boxers before reaching into his pocket and putting on his condom. He nudged her onto her back, his hands running over her breasts again, then down, taking hold of her underwear. He snapped it at the sides, pulling it off her in one fluid motion, and she squealed with laughter.

"You owe me a new pair," she said, as he held them up. He laughed, throwing them to one side before slipping his fingers between her legs. She reached down and caressed him, her hands moving in time with his strokes. Soon though, she was writhing and groaning under his hands, her voice becoming hoarser and hoarser.

"Is this your first time?" he whispered in her ear, nibbling her earlobe.

"Yes, yes," she gasped back and he rose over her, kneeling over her before gently nudging her legs apart. She reached up and caressed his cock, and he leaned in, gently sinking into her, giving her plenty of time to adjust to the pressure and depth he was sliding into her. She smiled, pulling him closer, gasping and crying out.

He slowly moved into her, rocking in and out, sliding and pushing gently. She soon arched into him, clutching at his hips, gasping and crying out as she moved under him. He leaned down, taking her breast in one hand, flicking at her nipple before sucking on it, holding it in his teeth. She cried out again and again, begging him to keep going, begging him not to stop.

She writhed under him, her hands gathering handfuls of sheets and more. He kept pushing faster and faster, as she rocked underneath him. She began spasming, pulsing underneath him, and crying out his name, and he kept going, loving the feel of her body around him, gasping and crying out.

He kept going, gently at first.

"Harder," she moaned, her skin slick with their sweat. He dived in, slamming into her harder and harder as she bucked and cried out underneath him, biting into his shoulder as he slammed into her again and again.

He spasmed and slammed into her, crying out her name, his hands clenching over hers and holding her down onto the bed, spilling into her as he rocked, slowing. She was still pulsing around him, her body clenching and unclenching around him.

She pulled him close, kissing his nose, and then relaxed underneath him. He lay on top of her for a minute or two, then sighed and pulled out. He padded off to the bathroom, while she lay for a minute, waiting for him.

On his return, she held up her ruined underwear and repeated, "You owe me a new pair."

"Second date then?" he asked.

8 ALAN'S BIG NIGHT OUT

21 September 2012.

First day at university and I'd already gathered fourteen phone numbers from hot girls in there with me. I can't believe it.

Alan Jackson's first day went as well as he'd expected: all the hot girls, swapping phone numbers and Facebook addresses, looking around at all of the short skirts and all of the pretty tops. He grinned. One or two of them were already heading for the student bar—he'd scoped that out the day before.

The 'intake' lectures and induction day were boring, so he spent the time looking for the girl to hone in on. Without being too obvious, he kept 'accidentally' sitting next to a pretty brunette that looked like she didn't have other friends. Her blue eyes looked down shyly, as he smiled and said hello. Eventually, he sat next to her and offered her a pen before she finished rooting in her bag.

"Here, have mine," he said, offering an equally shy smile and showing her his second one. She smiled at him and pulled out one of her own.

"Thanks, found it,"

She put her pen on the desk, pulled out an elaborately decorated folder, and plonked it down on the table too. It was a cacophony of photos. One in particular caught his eye—it and the note below it were intriguing.

@sexxy Becks, remember me when you wear 'the silk', Jaine.

He quirked an eyebrow, filing it away for another time.

She smiled over at him, following the path of his gaze. "My big sister is called Jaine," she explained, "and that photo was the first one I had taken after a car accident we were all in—on the beach to celebrate that we'd all come out relatively unscathed."

He nodded slowly, looking at the picture of her in a bikini. Lush, ripe curves and a taut stomach stared back.

"I'm Alan," he said, offering his hand. She took his hand and shook it.

"Becks," she said after a pause. He could see her considering whether to answer accurately or lie. He'd seen that look a lot these past few days.

"Short for Rebekah?" he asked.

"Short for Beckham actually," she said and he slapped his forehead with his palm. Laughing, she continued, "My name is Sophie, but everyone calls me Becks. It's even on the back of my sweatshirt," she added with a soft smile.

Her down-to-earth, friendly attitude made him even more interested in her, so boldly he said, "Would you like to come out for a pint tonight?"

"Oh, we're all going to Whitenoise," she said, as the lecturer walked in.

"Oh yeah, I might see you there then," he said with a grin.

Whitenoise, the local club, was run for students by 'older' students—at least in part. With a board made up of second and third years and an exclusive night for university goers, the club was one of the most popular in the area, and its demographic was firmly young, hot, and interesting.

Alan and his friends all went together, traveling in packs for comfort. Alan was determined to pull though— he'd been here for two weeks now and had his eye on several girls that had arrived in the last few days. He knew what he wanted and had fantasized already several times, one hand enclosed around his hot, hard cock.

He knew there were some nice girls— girls that he could probably pull easily, but he wanted to talk to Becks, wanted to take her to bed. But so far, he hadn't even seen her. There was no sign of her in the club, though it seemed like the whole university was out in force. He looked around—the dance floor was heaving with bodies, and the bar was three or four deep with students clamoring for the latest deals, the cheap drinks. He sighed and heaved himself into the throng, looking around to see if there was anyone else interesting.

And that was what he did for most of

the night.

The next class he would see her in was a week later. In the interim, he'd chatted to many girls, but he wanted to see Becks again. It turned out that they didn't share many classes either. Just two a week and only one was running from week one. So he didn't see her all week. He looked around the campus, of course, but he never saw her. The campus was full of thronging students—girls and boys sprinting between buildings.

Thursday was damp and wet. He wasn't expecting to see her, but there she was, tossing her hair over one shoulder, standing outside the classroom. Damp beads of water clung to the strands, falling over one shoulder, dripping down as she laughed and giggled with the other girls. There was a throng of them, waiting for the classroom to open.

He pushed his way past them and touched her arm. "Hi Becks," he said softly.

"Oh hi Alan!" she said, happily

turning to face him.

"Did you go to Whitenoise last week?"

"Yes…well…no. I went for a little while, and it was too busy so we went to Three Crows…"

"Oh right, the rock club?"

"Yeah. The deals there aren't as good, but it's a nicer club," she said. "We're going tonight. Wanna come?"

He could have cheered. "I'd love to," he said.

"How about I come to see you tonight before we go?" she said with a slight smile.

"Sure," he said, giving her his address.

He jumped in the shower, his frustrated hands wandering to his cock as he washed himself. He stroked hard as he stood in the shower, imagining plunging into Becks as he felt the lithe curves of her body under his arms. He imagined her sweet lips under his mouth. He devoured her in his mind, licking inside her lips. He groaned, holding himself up as his hands brought himself to climax, spilling all over himself and gasping as his body spasmed and shuddered. He turned the shower to cold, washing himself off as he got ready to go out.

He dressed and grabbed a beer from his fridge before collapsing to the couch before they went out. With an hour to go, he thought about what he wanted to do; it was one of the hardest waits he'd had for a while—worse than the first day.

She turned up fifteen minutes early, knocking on the door and calling his name. She sounded tipsy and giggly— and she was alone. He opened the door and she collapsed in a bit, giggling hard.

She held up her phone, showing him a lolcat image, before saying "Hi you!" and then adding, "I knocked on every door between the stairs and here." He looked out, three open doors looking at them, confused.

"Ah, that would be a problem. Come in?" He gestured towards his ratty couch bed. She grinned and flounced in.

"What are the chances of you fucking me?" she said, lying down on the couch, the edge of her skirt flipping up. He bit his lip and said, "Beer?"

She snorted and said, "I saw you watching me. I left my boyfriend before moving here, so...."

He didn't need to ask twice, slipping into the bathroom to grab a condom. When he returned, she had stripped to her underwear—the plain white lace stark against her skin. It was stretched tight across her hips, her long, black hair slipping over one shoulder and flowing off the edge of the bed. It was so easy to just drink in her beauty that he forgot to breathe for a minute.

"Will you come here and do me before my friends come looking for both of us?" she said, mock irritation in her words and on her lips. He laughed and stepped over to the sofa bed, dropping his trousers and moving towards her. She laughed, pulling her panties to one side and inviting him to take her with a smile.

He reached down, pulling them down and off, and then knelt on the bed and slipped into a condom while she slipped her finger into the damp area between her legs, the black curls shining with the damp edging her pleasure.

His mouth came up and licked one nipple through the satin of her bra. She groaned and pulled him down onto her—he sank into her with a grateful groan. There was a brief pause as she held her breath and then cried out, biting onto his shoulder. He reached over, grabbing some of her hair, feeling the silky hair slide under his fingertips. Pushing up from one side, he held himself up and stroked her arm. She trembled underneath him, biting her lip. He slipped his finger between them, rubbing her clitoris until she came all over him, the pulses driving him crazy. He slid in and out until he came too.

And then her phone rang.

Light fingers tickled over his skin as she returned from the phone call. "So, are we going to go?" she said.

"Do you mind if I ask who that was?"

"My mother," she said casually, gathering up her clothes and slipping back into them, wiggling and rearranging her breasts.

The nightclub was packed again and

she danced with him, occasionally dipping away like a butterfly every so often to go talk to her friends, then coming back and drinking from him with kisses and licks that made him want her all the more. Nearer the end of the night, she came to sit on his lap, hands entwined to his neck. There were a few people sitting like that, and many more were looking longingly around the room—hoping to pull. There was an air about the room, and as people drifted out and the DJ started playing less and less popular pieces, she looked down at him and said, "I want you to do me again, but first, I'd like to do something nice to you."

"Oh yeah?"

"Yeah," she said with a grin. She was drunk, wobbling on her heels, her breasts rubbing against his arm whenever she moved. It was difficult not to take her up a dark alley and slide into her there and then, but he held himself till they staggered back to the campus. Rowdy songs and joyous giggling followed them.

"Hungry?"

"Thanks," he said, pulling her closer,

his mouth reaching hers and kissing her hungrily. His tongue nudged her lips and her mouth and licked the teeth and the sensitive insides of her mouth. She was still slightly cold, but he was enjoying the taste of her on his tongue. He groaned again and rubbed her arms, her skin covered in goose bumps, her muscles trembling. She was so cold that he decided to give her his jacket so that her arms weren't bare any more. The cool October air touched her skin and made her shiver. She snuggled gratefully, her arms wrapping around his side, pulling in close. His shirt was so thin that he could feel her breath on his shoulder.

"So...more fun?" he asked.

She laughed. "One day at a time, sunshine," she said with a happy, drunken smile. He grinned back at her, slipping his hand up inside her lace top, running it up on the bare skin at her back and slipping his finger under her bra strap. He found a rough patch and she laughed, "That tickled," she said. "It's a scrape where I fell while I was at the gym," she said and he removed his fingers.

"I've got scrapes like that from my

cat," he said with a careful smile. There was nothing left to say after that; his fingers explored the chilled skin at her back, smiling as he found something nice to stroke, to feel, sliding around across her rib cage.

The walk to her flat—that she shared with three other girls—felt like it went on forever. Alan wasn't sure where he was—he hadn't really explored this end of the town. What he did know was that everything was within walking distance and he liked that. It was a comfort in many ways and was easy to know that he wasn't going to get lost.

The flat was even more beaten up than the student dorms. The stained, ratty carpet under his feet was rough and sticky; she made him take his shoes off at the door and they pantomimed quietly while falling over everything in her way herself. One flatmate finally stuck her head around the corner and said, "Oh, Becks, c'mon. I've got classes at 9:15. Oh hi...Alan right?"

Alan looked surprised and then looked closer. The plain blonde girl with her hair in a mess was the sleek girl who sat next to him in one of his law classes. He laughed softly.

"Hi Jessica," he said, not sure whether to be embarrassed, annoyed, or amused.

"She's pissed," she observed and Alan nodded.

"You missed a good night," he said.

"I'll see you at class tomorrow? Or want me to take notes?" she said, winking, before ducking back into the room behind her.

Becks pulled him up the hall as his jaw worked. He hadn't worked out what to say, but Becks was pulling resolutely, leading him towards the door at the very end of the hall. When they got there, she drunkenly tried to open the door before he closed his hand around hers, sighing slightly, "You're really drunk. Shall I go home and see you?"

She pulled him close, her hand finding her way to his pants and stroking his cock through his jeans. It almost instantly hardened, the material tightening across the bulge. He sighed and followed her into the room.

The room itself was dominated by a

metal bedstead and a tiny chest of drawers. Clothes and other items were scattered everywhere, and he fell through the door with a loud "oof" and pulled her into a heap with him.

They both laughed for a bit before she pantomimically shushed him and pulled him into the room so she could close the door. Then, stripping of all her clothes, she threw herself across the bed like a blanket and said, "I'm all yours."

"What was the surprise?" he asked, throwing his clothes all over the floor.

She laughed, clapping her hands over her mouth.

"I was going to BLOW you," she said with mock solemnity. "But I'm too drunk. It'll have to wait till morning," she added.

Mentally, he thought about his timetable and looked at the clock. It was 3 a.m. No way was he going to get that tomorrow morning and make classes.

"Fuck me again?" she asked. He shook his head.

"How about I just pleasure you?" he said, and she grinned.

"How about we do one another," she

said and pushed him flat on his back. She climbed on him, straddling him, before taking his cock in her mouth. Alan groaned, straining up—his bare skin was wet from her mouth as she let go and said, "Either I can blow you, or we can do each other, your call."

He leaned forward slightly, licking her pussy, and she shuddered. He brought his hands up, parting her lips and finding her clitoris, lashing his lounge across it with practiced ease. She dropped her head back into his lap, groaning occasionally around his cock as she sucked and licked, cupping his balls with one hand, providing regular strokes with the other. He licked and invaded her with his lounge, trying to keep control as she brought him closer and closer to orgasm. Eventually he begged, "Stop...stop please," and she laughed.

He continued to lick her while she hovered over him, groaning and tossing her head back. When he'd cooled a little, she began to suck on him again until once again, he was begging for her to stop. His hands ran over her round ass, enjoying the silky feel of the skin under his fingers before lightly stroking down her thighs.

"I want to kiss you," he demanded, and she laughed again, the silvery sound causing him to shiver as her breath blew onto his bare skin and over his cock. His hands moved further up, stroking her breasts, reaching up to caress her before she turned to him and shook her head.

She turned around, pulled a condom from the little jar under her bed, and carefully slipped it onto his cock. He gasped again as she sank onto him, sitting upright and playing with her clit while he watched. She was on the verge of ecstasy, her loud moans making him laugh and pull her down towards him. Carefully and slowly, he began thrusting up into her, moving with her as she rocked her hips, his hands finding her nipples and pulling them to his mouth, guiding the whole breast closer to him.

His hands stroked her as she rocked, her teeth biting his neck lightly and sucking. He was sure she was leaving love bites, but he enjoyed it so much such that it caused tingles of lighting to shoot down his arms and legs as he thrust harder and harder. His hands found her hair again, tangling in it as her mouth pressed down on his, tasting and tormenting him as she bucked and shivered as he thrust harder and faster. Her moans only pushed him on; her hands were all over him, her mouth finding his nipples before traveling back up to his neck, her wet tongue slipping over his chilled skin.

She came all over him violently, her whole body quaking as he took her deeper and deeper, sinking right to the root of his penis, and that pushed him over the edge. Hoarsely, he yelped and spasmed harder and harder until his whole body twitched and shuddered.

They came to a stop, kissing and stroking for a while before falling asleep draped across one another, their hands entangled in each other's bodies.

Far too quickly, 6 am came. Alan got up to pee and to clean himself up and then snuck back to bed with Becks. She was sleeping soundly, snoring softly. He ran his hand over her bare back, the chill settling on her skin like a nightdress. Pulling her blanket over them both, he snuggled in for a few minutes before wondering if he should get up and let himself out. He debated what to do until he heard her flatmates waking up and moving around; he then casually dressed and excused himself, leaving a note for her before he did. The girls were all catcalling and wolf-whistling on his way out of the door and he blushed profusely.

Once he got his bearings and found his way back to the flat, he found that a shower, a shave, and a cup of coffee made him feel much closer to human. But he wasn't going to make it to first class. Knowing her flatmate would take the mickey when she saw him next, he decided to take it on the chin. He sloped off to class, arriving a couple of minutes late, and was amused to see the said flatmate looking a little worse for wear. The professor told them to grab some cups of coffee as this was an informal class, so everyone headed to the refectory and grabbed some beverages. Alan took the opportunity to down some energy drinks—and was suddenly more awake.

When his phone rang, he answered it, walking out of the refectory and back to class.

"Awwww...I woke up this morning and you were gone," she said. He could almost hear the pout in her voice.

"Classes," he said wryly. She laughed softly.

"And here I am in this nice, warm, empty bed..."

"I'm done in an hour," he said, hopefully.

"Oh, I might be up and be at the coffee shop by then, but if you phone me..."

"Or I could just come back now?"

"You could. I had a lot of fun last night," she said, and he could hear the coy charm in her voice. He laughed softly.

"I'll come to see you in a few hours," he said.

"Phone me first?"

"Sure."

After class, he phoned and she answered quickly. He knew she was keen to have him over; he could hear it in her voice. The one-off pull that he'd hoped to make was quickly turning into something much better—he couldn't believe his luck.

"Hi Becks! I said I'd call after class."

"So you did," she said, sounding a bit cooler towards him. "What are you doing for the rest of the day?"

"Active learning seminar, then I was going to go out for pizza with a few friends. Why?"

"Done the active learning stuff already," she said, sounding disappointed.

"I've got an hour yet," Alan said, smiling to himself.

"Oh good! Wanna meet me at the house?"

He bounded up the stairs three at a time, two coffees from the little shop downstairs in hand. He tapped on her door and was surprised when her flatmate opened it—one that he hadn't met before. He hesitated, before asking, "Is Becks around?"

"Oh, yes, she's in her room. Come on in," the redhead said, opening the door. He noticed an abandoned Hoover outside Becks' room and smiled.

"BECKS!" the girl yelled and he

jumped, "Company."

"Thanks Dar!" she yelled back, her voice muffled by the door. She opened it, revealing a pretty sundress rolled down so she could tan across her shoulders, the window to the small roof, which was mostly flat outside her window, open.

"Hi!" she said and kissed him. He grinned again, feeling self-conscious. "How was class?"

"Dull, but I can see it getting exciting soon," he said.

She laughed. "Can I borrow your notes? I should have been there, but I forgot." She looked brazen and unrepentant and winked at him as he closed the door.

"Oh, I guess...what am I getting in return?"

She crossed the room in a flash, pinning him up against the door and kissing him.

"How about you being handcuffed to the bed and kinky stuff being done to you?" she asked, looking slightly embarrassed.

He laughed. "Sure...I didn't say that too fast, did I?"

She laughed hard. "No, you didn't,"

she said with a smile.

She led him to the bed and he noticed the handcuffs. They were dangling from the bedposts and sparkled in the mid-morning light coming through the window.

"Strip then," she ordered and gestured to the bed again. He laughed softly and did as he was told. A hint of nervousness crossed his mind then—what if she left him handcuffed there and got photos, or called in her roommates?

And then she stripped too before cuffing one hand and then the other to the bed. She pulled out some oil and a condom and smiled at him.

He admired the lace underwear in front of him—burgundy, scarlet, and violet; it was deep and rich against her pale, slightly tanned skin. He was also surprised to note that she had no tan lines—her skin was of the same even tone all over.

She bent her head, her glossy black hair falling over her shoulder and onto his stomach as she kissed a line from his pelvis up over his stomach, diverting slightly to take one nipple in her mouth, then the other. He groaned, pulling against the cuffs slightly, and she laughed.

"Sit back and enjoy it," she told him softly, then took the other nipple in her hand. Meanwhile, she got some oil out, heating it slightly before dribbling it on his stomach. He gasped, the slight chill still in the oil working against the heat rising off his skin. She massaged it in, spreading it across his stomach and up his chest before turning and working on his thighs and calves. The deep tissue massage was relaxing and made him groan and stretch; it made him want to try to kiss her leg or thigh as it came near his mouth. She simply giggled and kept going.

After some time, she took the condom out of its wrapper and took it in her mouth. Carefully, with exaggerated movements, she slowly lowered it onto his dick, holding it in place with her tongue as she moved it down his shaft. He grunted and arched his back, intense pleasure flowing through him as she caressed and licked his cock until she was satisfied with the results. By this point, he was panting and begging, his hands pulling against the cuffs.

"I could just leave you here," she told him. "Classes and all that," she added. He laughed.

"You'd come back for me though, right?"

"Maybe yes, maybe no," she said and reached over him, climbing on top of him. He realized she wasn't wearing any knickers and she slid onto him smoothly. He arched into her and she smiled again, his skin tingling, his hands desperate to catch and capture her... to hold and feel her in his arms... to pull her closer. She smiled and nodded at the cuffs.

"Want out?"

He nodded his head, "Yes please, Becks."

"Tough," she said with a giggle, rocking slightly as she moved against him. She played with her breasts, rubbing her wet fingers over her nipples and then slowly working her way down into the damp thatch of hair between her legs. Moaning, she began to play with herself, bringing herself to orgasm on him as he watched. He found it unbearable that he couldn't join in or play with her—that he wasn't allowed to do anything to her. His hands itched to be free to find and cup her breasts and to feel her moving underneath him and on top of him, as they both found pleasure. His skin was on fire—every touch an intense shot of pleasure through his system and every breath an amazingly pleasurable experience. He moved with her, rocking as carefully as he could, arching into her and falling back, pulling on his handcuffs before finally, she began to pulse and squeal around him. Her body got filled with shuddering, shivering spasms and she came all over him, squealing out his name, begging him to thrust deeper. He complied and moved into her and pushed harder. She ground down on him, breathing heavily, pulsing around his cock, and suddenly he couldn't take it anymore and he came too, slamming up and jerking and bucking into her. They shuddered together for a bit before she ducked her head, taking his nipple into her mouth again, causing him to shake, shudder, and wiggle underneath her.

"That...that tickles!" he said.

She laughed. "In a good way, right?"

"Yes," he said and wiggled. "You're

going to uncuff me?"

"No...," she said, eyes sparkling, before continuing, "I really like having you as captive here." She giggled and removed the handcuffs. He pulled her down, kissing her before saying, "C'mon, classes again soon." She sighed, and then laughed.

9 MAGIC AT THE CLUB MAGIQUE

The club was thumping—a deep bass pump which fell in time with his heart. He looked around, his mouth dry. He wished he'd grabbed a pint on the way across the room, but the bar had been heaving, and his first thought was for his girlfriend, who'd invited him here. She'd been brought by her poly alt-partner and loved it, and now she told him, quietly, at the meal the night before, "We have to go. You'll love it."

The room was full of people dressed in various garbs—everything from simple corsetry to full on gimp outfits— he felt kind of underdressed in his shirt and leather trousers, but she'd told him that he'd be fine. And he'd believed her—the deep noise in his chest echoed into his soul and bound him. He began to feel excited as he saw rooms edging this side of the room— flashes of bare skin and people tumbling around on the beds in the room. Men and women held in ecstasy, moving with one another—two and three of them to a room. Some rooms held men watching two women playing with one another—others had men playing with women looking on. Some were just two people, their limbs a blur and mess of movement and passion.

He looked for his girlfriend—she'd told him that she was behind a green curtain, after two red, when coming from the bar. Finally, he thought he found her—sprawled on a bed with the curtains open. Men were walking slowly past the door, looking in to see her tied lightly to the bed with a scarf. Another woman sat, nearer the door, making sure no one entered until she saw Peter.

"There you are," she murmured, reaching up and stroking his face. "I've been guarding your beloved," she added, then nudged him inside.

"Hi?" he said. He wasn't expecting a threesome and cautiously watched her. She smiled.

"Strip," she said. Her leather corset sparkled, and he realised that she'd been sitting under a black veil, watching his girlfriend. She was still dressed, but was lying supine, her legs slightly apart and relaxed.

"Ok?" he said, and as he began to carefully shrug out of his clothes, she closed the curtains. Once closed, some of the sound was also blocked out—he couldn't believe that it was much quieter, but there it was. She reached behind an alcove curtain and pulled out a blindfold, before waiting patiently for him to strip to his underwear.

"Leave that for now," she said, then blindfolded him, pulling him over to the bed. He was already excited, erect and ready to play with his girlfriend— the frisson of someone being in the same room while they had sex, plus the idea that people could walk in on them excited him more than he could explain and he willingly submitted to blindfolding. The woman in the room laughed and whispered, "She's been waiting patiently for you—hasn't even let me..." she paused, running a nail down his bare back, "pleasure her." He blinked and smiled at her, and she ran her finger around the waistband of his shorts; his girlfriend smiling and watching, tied and still, from the bed. He couldn't believe it—she'd told him there was a surprise waiting but he didn't expect this.

The second woman was slightly older and watched him carefully as he stood, before finally saying, "I am her mistress. As such, she belongs to me. And she brought you," she ran her hands into his shorts, "As a gift. I think I will be kind and give you back tonight. Should you return though..." she finished with a smile and he nodded.

"You will do as I say," she added. "Your shorts will be removed in bed," she said, looking him over with a self-satisfied smile.

He shivered, and waited patiently, feeling naked even though he still wore his boxer shorts. She gently led him to the bed, easing him onto the area beside her. He reached out, stroking her skin, moving down to explore her corset, working his way down to her underwear. Hooking his fingers under the knickers, he snuck his fingers into the damp curls underneath.

He heard the woman say, "I'll untie you now," and his girlfriend laugh.

Suddenly, she was pushing him over onto his back, tying his hands, leaving him blind and unable to move. A set of hands began rubbing his muscles, moving up from his ankles to his thighs, stopping before reaching his pelvis. Another set, he was sure, began to pull his underwear off, gently pulling his hips up and removing his underwear. He gasped, the colder air touching his skin, the sweat moving off his skin and rapidly cooling. He wiggled, saying, "Where are you?"

"Shsssh," his girlfriend replied. A mouth began to kiss his shoulder, working her way down to his nipple. He yelped as her mouth met his nipple and another reached over and kissed him.

"Who's there?" he asked. Both girls laughed, the softer voice of his girlfriend followed by the slightly deeper voice of the girl "guarding" the room where his girlfriend lay.

He relaxed, feeling very self-conscious, his skin tingling as he waited for the next hand, the next kiss. A mouth met his, licking his lips, as he lay blindfolded and tied to the bed. Another hand carefully reached down and tied one ankle to the bed, then the other. Spread-eagled, they began to lavish attention on him, one taking him in her mouth, the other moving down and stroking and caressing his balls. A breast brushed his cheek and he turned his head, seeking the nipple. A woman gasped as he did—he couldn't tell if it was his girlfriend or her friend.

Hands stroked his arms, caressing him—feeling his skin under their fingertips. He laughed—the tickling sensation causing him to tremble before gasping again as he was sucked and licked and caressed to orgasm. He came and felt the warmth of it flow over his lower stomach. The girls laughed and then sat over him, either side of him. He could feel them reaching across him to stroke and kiss one another, and after a minute, his girlfriend reached up and took the blindfold off, before continuing to lavish attention on the woman across his body from her. They cleaned him up first, before returning their attention to each other, warm towels wiping him from head to foot. His cock twitched slightly when she gently cleaned him, finishing the job with another suckle and lick. He raised his hips involuntarily, trying to get to her. Ashe just laughed, and returned to what she was doing—her hands reached over and stroked heavy breasts, her smaller ones lit by flickering candlelight. He groaned again, his orgasm still shuddering through him slightly, as the girls brought each other close to climax. He felt himself twitch again, and they both smiled, reaching over again to stroke one another.

"I...I want you," he told them both and his girlfriend laughed. She brought her friend to orgasm—she came near his face, near enough that he could feel the shuddering twitch of her muscles, and she withdrew. She sat down at the bottom of the bed, facing away from them, apparently enthralled in replacing and rearranging her corsetry. His girlfriend deftly slipped a condom on him, before running her hands over his chest, taking a nipple in his mouth, and straddling him. His skin tingled with a fire as she slid onto him, his body aching to feel her orgasm around him.

"I waited all night for you," she whispered to him, her breath hot and fragrant against his ear. He sighed, pulling against the bonds of the bed, and she laughed and continued, "Though, you don't seem too worried about threesomes, just being tied to the bed. Are you feeling vulnerable?" she finished and he laughed.

"Not really—never been to one of these clubs before, I really didn't know what to expect,"

"It's never the same twice," she told him, sliding onto his cock. She groaned and moaned as she slid him inside her, the heat enveloping him as she sunk onto him. He arched his back slightly, pushing up into her until he was as deep as she could take him and she slowly began moving against him, pulsing up and down as she brought herself to orgasm. It was powerful and crushing—his skin tingling and shivering as he felt her cum all over him. He was wet and slick with her juices, her orgasm causing her to tremble and collapse onto him. He rocked into her as she murmured and yelped, his orgasm following closely behind her. This one tore through him, the pleasure of feeling her cum around him overtaking him as he slammed into her, crying out hoarsely. He was suddenly glad for the loud music—the noise of his orgasm tearing from his lips.

Finally, they lay still, in the bed, a light blanket covering them as she nibbled on his shoulder and skin.

"Wanna dance?" she finally asked.

10 THREE, TWO, ONE

I watched my boyfriend bring his girlfriend hesitantly into the room. She was a slight, petite girl, matching his slim build—almost androgynous. She wore a dress that clung to the few curves she had—but now that it was removed, I could tell that she was uncomfortable and shy. Her arms were hunched in and across her barely-there breasts, her skin a milky white against the black I'd chosen for her. This had been something we'd arranged over the past few weeks—each of us choosing an element. She'd chosen the house (ours), Max chose her restraints (leather cuffs) and I'd chosen her underwear (black, lacy and front fastening).

She seemed nervous and was being led by a set of cuffs that he'd obviously put on her once she'd taken her dress off. We'd been out for a meal that evening, each of us looking around nervously. We'd arranged this in our private chat room—I'd met her before of course—they'd been dating for a year now and he'd suggested it.

There was a suggestion of an open relationship in the offing about three months before. And we'd talked it to death. Max and I were old friends— uni-buddies who'd stayed together after leaving our wild days behind us; he'd met Rachel and things had cooled between us, till she met me. There was this...gleam in her eye when she first met me—as if she was sizing me up. I didn't doubt he'd told her our history, so it was much easier just to slide into whatever came next. We'd been flat mates and on and off lovers for a while, so the suggestion of a threesome wasn't exactly a problem.

He led her to the bed and I stripped,

making sure I put on a condom straight away. We all stood around the bed, looking at one another, until she sighed and with a giggle said:

"Me first I guess?" She sat, owl eyed, but excited, watching us both speculatively as I joined her on the bed. Finally, Max stripped and joined us, sliding a condom on as she lay down, hands above her head. They weren't hooked to anything, but she was cuffed now.

"Shall we both play with you?" he asked and she shook her head.

"Play with each other, I'll watch..." she said, with a soft smile. "Uncuff me though?"

Max's smile was wicked. "Not yet. I know how you feel about watching and not getting involved—it really turns you on. I think we'll do that at first." He said, and reached for me. I could see she was tormented by this—her pout was half disappointed, half playful, but she lay back, watching. Her hands twitched above her head and after a time, she reached down, across her body, and slid her fingers into her underwear. Having both hands tied didn't seem to slow her down any—she closed her eyes and began to pleasure herself, groaning softly. Max looked over, before turning his attention back to me. I was already turned on—the sight of Max stripping and then joining her on the bed was almost too much for me to take.

We kissed roughly, hands all over one another's bodies, exploring and reclaiming. I was always vaguely jealous of him when he came home from spending time with Rachel—there was something about the idea of someone else touching his skin that made me possessive. I devoured his skin, tasting his sweat, smelling him and enjoying him as I roughly flipped him over, taking him from behind. She took great pleasure in this, reaching over with her cuffed hands to stroke him, before moving so that she could suck on his cock as I took him from behind.

Max was in ecstasy—unsure what to do, he caressed her breasts as she sucked him off and I fucked him from behind. It wasn't the original idea of what we'd planned to do, but seemed the most natural position to get him into.

"Don't let him cum," I told her, withdrawing from his quivering ass before I did and she smiled and stopped. He looked back at me, disappointed, before rocking back and sitting down on his haunches.

"Why did you do that?" he mock demanded, with a laugh. She sighed and shook her head, winking at me. We all stopped for some sips of wine, and she grabbed an ice cube and began tracing our muscles with it. We both laughed, and, looking at one another, also grabbed an ice cube from the bucket, running it up and round her nipples—the dark mounds tightening and protruding as she fell back with a pleasured gasp. Max winked at me, running one down her stomach, between her legs and she yelped again, as he circled her lips with it.

He shook and trembled for a minute, before turning and roughly kissing me, then pushed me back and off the bed and I sat in a chair, watching them both. Voyeurism was new to me, but I found myself unbearably turned on—taking myself in my hand, I began to stroke as I watched her bring my lover closer and closer to release. Her mouth worked over his nipples, leaving slight smears of lipstick and glistening trails as she licked and caressed him. They were kneeling, his cock pushing into her thighs and resting there, perhaps feeling the dampness at her core.

He flipped her onto her back, pushing her down and lavishing attention on her breasts, sucking and kissing her nipples. Her cries were enticing, and I gently reached down and peeled off the condom, wrapping it and tossing it in the bin before beginning to gently stroke and explore my body. He uncuffed her hands, pulling them off and tossing them onto the floor before stripping her of her bra and panties, the light curls a contrast to his dark head. He ducked his head, taking her in his mouth and sucking on her clit until she screamed and yelped, tipping her hips and moving with him as he brought her closer and closer to climax. Her cries were making me tingle—I wanted to experience the taste and feel of her skin underneath my lips, so I joined them on the bed.

"May I?" I asked. Dizzy with pleasure, swollen lips smiling softly, she reached up and pulled me down into the jumble of arms and legs, kissing and stroking my face. I sat back and grabbed a new condom from the bedside table, before sliding it down onto my hard, twitching cock, stroking Max's ass before allowing her to take me in her mouth. I groaned, the pleasure almost palpable and involuntarily twitched as she caressed and stroked. She was groaning too, every so often, she'd moan around my cock as Max moved down and did more things to her, his tongue invading her core and washing over her clit. He was putty in her hands, as she stroked his cock. I reached over too, closing my hand over hers and we both stroked her for a bit, and Max was once again almost insensible with pleasure. I loved doing that to him, taking him to the edge before pulling back and letting him cool, before starting all over again.

We stopped as he begged us to and he went back to lavishing attention on her clit—his tongue penetrating and drawing out her pleasure. I wanted to do so too, but there wasn't room—instead, I took one soft, dark nipple into my mouth, drawing it out and rolling it across my lips and along my tongue. She wiggled and gasped, her hands coming up and entwining in my hair.

Soon, she was writing and moving underneath him, and I was close to orgasm again, my whole body shaking and twitching under her tongue's ministrations. I couldn't believe how differently she turned me on—her deft licks and strokes seemed more in time with my body than even I was.

Finally, he slipped into her, rocking and slamming as she continued to pleasure me. He reached over and stroked me, heightening the pleasure, while I ran my hands over her slightly soft stomach, and up over her ribcage. Her breasts were small but firm—the soft curves under my hands a welcome change to the harder muscles I was used to feeling. Her skin was soft, with a peachy fuzz—warm and tense under our gentle ministrations. She began to shudder as Max reached climax—calling out both of our names. She soon followed, and that drove me over the edge—I exploded and poured into the condom, in her mouth as she came all over Max, who came inside her. The tingle was too much to bear and we collapsed on top of each other, a tangle of sweating, shuddering limbs.

"Again?" Max eventually managed and we all laughed.

AUTHOR'S NOTE

Readers: I want to expand a few of the stories to see where the characters can be explored further. If there are any of the stories that you would like to read more about again, I'd love to hear from you!

Visit my blog at http://www.dakotadeece.com

Join my newsletter for free exclusive previews
http://www.dakotadeece.com/in

Follow me on Twitter at
http://www.twitter.com/dakotadeece

Like my page on Facebook at
http://www.facebook.com/dakotadeece

Discover my books at major ebook retailers everywhere.

www.ingramcontent.com/pod-product-compliance
Lightning Source LLC
Chambersburg PA
CBHW020742130626
46554CB00006B/2100